SESAME STREET

Bert and Ernie's Great Adventures

Ooga-Booga Dinosaurs!

Adapted by Kathryn Knight from the script by Luis Santeiro

LEVEL **1** READER

READING LEVEL

Published by Dalmatian Press, LLC. All rights reserved.
Printed in Guangzhou, Guangdong, China.

The DALMATIAN PRESS name is a trademark of Dalmatian Publishing Group.
Franklin, Tennessee 37068-2068. 1-866-418-2572.
No part of this book may be reproduced or copied in any form without written permission
from the copyright owner. CE13029/1211

"Og ooga-booga!
Og bog bood!
We are cave men
looking for food!"

Bert rubbed his tummy.
"I am hungry, Ernie," he said.
"Where can we eat?"

"We will go look," said Ernie.
"We must make our food here.
This is the land of dinosaurs."

Rummm-rumble-RUMBLE!

"What is that?"
Bert asked Ernie.

"It must be my tummy,"
said Ernie.
"I am hungry, too."

Ernie looked
and looked.
Oh, my! Look at that!
"Bert!" he called.
"Look at the big eggs."

"Og-tastic!" said Bert.
"We can take an egg.
We can cook it."
"Yes!" said Ernie.

Bert looked at the egg.
"It is big," he said.
"How will we get it
   to the cave?"

"I will call
   for help,"
   said Ernie.
"TAXI!"

"That is so silly," said Bert.
"There is no taxi here."

Beep! Beep! ZWING!
"Meet my friend,"
said Ernie.
"His name is Taxi."

Wheeeee!
Taxi swung in the trees.
Wheeeee!
Taxi took them
to the cave.
"Thank you," said Ernie.
"Ugg," said Taxi.

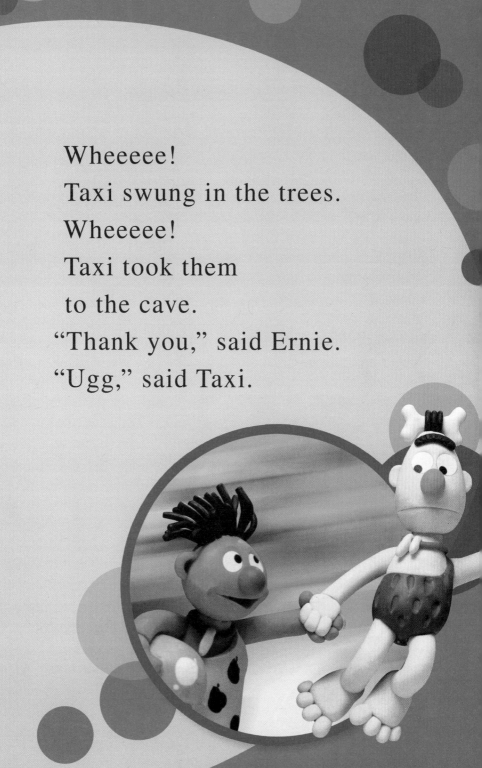

"I will cook," said Bert.
"I will cook us an ooga-egg."

Ernie did not hear.
He was singing.
"Ooga woo! Booga wah!
Ooga woo! Booga wah!"

The egg wiggled.
The egg wobbled.
Crack!

"What is that?"
Bert asked Ernie.

Ernie did not hear.
"Ernie!" called Bert.
"Did you hear . . . ?"

CRRACKK!

"AAAAGH!"
yelled Bert.
It was a baby!
A baby dinosaur!

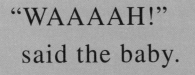

"WAAAAH!"
said the baby.

Ernie looked up.
"Look, Bert," he said.
"It is a baby dinosaur."

"Yes," said Bert.
"I *see* it is a dinosaur."

The baby jumped
into Bert's arms.
"Mama?" it asked.

"Oh, no!" said Ernie.
"Where is the mama?
That dinosaur is little,
but the mama will be . . ."

Bert and Ernie hopped
into a cave car.
Zoom zoom zoom
went the car.

Stomp stomp stomp
went the big dinosaur.

The car was fast.
The dinosaur was faster!

"I will call for help,"
said Ernie.
"TAXI!"

Beep! Beep!
ZWING!

Wheeeee!
Taxi took them to
the top of a tall rock.
"Thank you," said Ernie.
"Ugg," said Taxi.

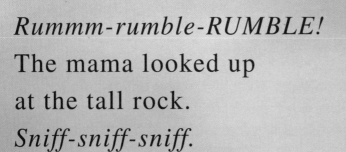

Rummm-rumble-RUMBLE!
The mama looked up
at the tall rock.
Sniff-sniff-sniff.

"Oh, Ernie," said Bert,
"look how *sad* she is."

The baby looked
at the big dinosaur.
"Mama?" it asked.

"That is your mama," said Bert.
He took the baby.
He sat the baby on
the mama's nose.